Meena Fernald

PQ-DOO-888

Meena Fernald

THE RAINBOW TULIP

BY

PAT MORA

ILLUSTRATED BY

ELIZABETH SAYLES

VIKING

VIKING
Published by the Penguin Group
Penguin Putnam Books for Young Readers, 345 Hudson Street, New York, New York 10014, U.S.A.
Penguin Books Ltd, 27 Wrights Lane, London W8 5TZ, England
Penguin Books Australia Ltd, Ringwood, Victoria, Australia
Penguin Books Canada Ltd, 10 Alcorn Avenue, Toronto, Ontario, Canada M4V 3B2
Penguin Books (N.Z.) Ltd, 182-190 Wairau Road, Auckland 10, New Zealand

Penguin Books Ltd, Registered Offices: Harmondsworth, Middlesex, England

First published in 1999 by Viking, a member of Penguin Putnam Books for Young Readers.

1 3 5 7 9 10 8 6 4 2

LIBRARY OF CONGRESS CATALOGING-IN-PUBLICATION DATA
Mora, Pat.
The rainbow tulip / by Pat Mora ; illustrated by Elizabeth Sayles.
p.   cm.
Summary: A Mexican-American first-grader experiences the difficulties and pleasures of being different
when she wears a tulip costume with all the colors of the rainbow for the school May Day parade.
ISBN 0-670-87291-1 (hc.)
1. Mexican Americans—Juvenile fiction. [1. Mexican Americans—
Fiction. 2. May Day—Fiction. 3. Schools—Fiction.] I. Sayles,
Elizabeth, ill. II. Title. PZ7.M78819Rai 1999 [E]—dc21 98-15868 CIP AC

Printed in Hong Kong
Set in Goudy

For my first editor, my wonderful mother, Estela Mora
—P. M.

To my grandparents, Fannie, Nathan, Bessie, and Alexander,
who long ago made the long journey to America
—E. S.

Every morning my mother gives me a huge spoonful of thick, yellow cod liver oil. She thinks I am too thin. She says a strong desert wind could blow me away.

My brothers and I eat breakfast with my mother and father before I go to school. I'm the oldest.

My father gives us an *abrazo*, a hug, and says, "*Buenos días, hijos.*" My mother and father came to this country from Mexico. They don't speak English.

My brothers and I speak English outside the house and Spanish inside the house. My father says, "*Hija*, this house is a piece of Mexico."

At home I'm Estelita. At school my name is Stella. My mother walks me to school. She likes to hold my hand.

I say, "*Mamá*, I can walk to school by myself. I am big now. I am in first grade."

"*Sí, sí, Estelita*," my mother says, but she holds my hand tighter.

My mother is not like the other mothers. Our neighbors all speak English. They do not speak Spanish like my mother. She does not wear makeup. Her hair is tied in a bun, and her dresses are long. My mother does not wear colors that sing and dance. My mother likes to wear black, brown, gray, sometimes light blue. My mother is quiet like her colors.

"*Mamá*," I say, "when I am big, I will buy red dresses."

"*Ay, que muchacha*," chuckles my mother. "Oh, what a girl."

"I will," I say. "I will buy red shiny shoes and hats with feathers. I will buy green dresses and purple dresses. I will have all the colors in my closet."

"*Sí, sí*," says my mother, laughing her quiet laugh.

I like my school very much. I like my friends and my teacher,
Mrs. Douglas. She likes me, too. I always raise my hand to
answer questions. Mrs. Douglas lets me erase the blackboard
after school. My mother and her smile are always waiting for me.

At home, my brothers and I run races with our neighbors. When I'm hungry, I go inside. My house is a quiet house. My father likes to read his books. Outside, my brothers and I shout and run, but inside, we do not shout.

While my mother cooks, I eat lime sherbet, very slowly. The lime sherbet is sweet and sour. It slides down my throat. I eat it slowly, very slowly so that it will last longer.

"Ay, *que muchacha*," says my mother, patting my hand.

One day my teacher says, "Soon our class will be in the May parade. The girls will be tulips. The boys will wear white shirts and nice trousers. Please take this letter home to your parents. It tells them what you'll need."

Walking home, I say, "*Mamá*, I need a tulip costume."

"We can go visit your aunt, Tía Carmen, who sews beautiful dresses," says my mother. "Do you want to be a yellow tulip, Estelita?"

"No," I say.

"Do you want to be a pink tulip?" asks my mother.

"No," I say.

"Estelita, what color tulip do you want to be?" she asks.

"I want to be a yellow tulip and a pink tulip and a green tulip and a purple tulip," I say. "I want all the spring colors in my costume."

We visit my aunt who makes bride dresses and party dresses. "*Buenas tardes, Tía Carmen,*" I say, giving her an *abrazo*. She shows me her rainbows of threads and clouds of cloth. She measures me and tells me that I will be the most beautiful tulip, *el tuipán más lindo,* in the whole world, *en todo el mundo.*

At school our teacher shows us how to weave a Maypole. She asks if our tulip costumes are almost ready. I nod yes.

The day of the May parade, I wake up before anyone in the house. I slip into my costume. I look at myself in the mirror and smile.

I eat my breakfast standing up. I don't want to wrinkle my petals. My brothers say I look funny. My father frowns at the boys, and they get very quiet. My father was a judge in Mexico. My father never yells, but when he looks at you, you behave. I smile at my *papá*. He likes my costume.

My mother hands me a sweater. My mother always thinks it's cold. "Ay, *Mamá*," I say. "I cannot cover my costume. I want everyone to see it. Let's go. *Vámonos*."

I see my friends waving at me in the playground, but I do not look like they look. Betsy is a yellow tulip. Louise is a pink tulip. Frances is a blue tulip. I feel quiet as a snail inside. My hands feel very hot. I wave good-bye to my mother.

My friends and I say, "Oh, you look so pretty. Oh, you look so pretty," but I feel quiet as a snail inside.

I am afraid to see my teacher's face. What if she laughs at me? What if she wants to talk to my mother? I walk slowly into the room.

My teacher is very busy. When she looks at me, she says, "Stella is our rainbow tulip," and she smiles. Some of the boys laugh. I try to smile, but my smile is hiding.

When it's time for the parade, we peek out the windows and see mothers and fathers in the playground. I look for my mother. I know that she will stand alone because she cannot talk to the other parents.

The school band starts to play, and we march to the playground. The parents all clap. I see some people point at my
rainbow costume. I try to smile.

When I pass by my mother, she reaches out to hand me my
sweater. "*Estelita, hace frío*," she says. "It is cold."

I push the sweater away. I wish my mother would learn English. I wish she looked like the other mothers with their makeup and short dresses.

We start to weave the Maypole. Everyone is watching us. I see my little brothers watching me. I can't let them see I'm scared. I'm the oldest.

Then I see my mother and her quiet smile. I know she is proud of me, and I stand very straight. I smile at her, too. I remember every step of the dance. I help my friends who forget what to do. I see my teacher smiling at me. I see the principal smiling at me. When the class bows, my mother claps and claps.

My teacher puts her arm around me. "Stella," she says, "you are my only rainbow tulip."

I bring my mother to meet my teacher. My teacher says, "How do you do, Mrs. Delgado." My mother nods and smiles her quiet smile. I wish my teacher could speak Spanish. I wish she could tell my mother that I always raise my hand at school.

The wind is cool. I put on the sweater my mother brought for me. It feels soft and warm. I take my mother's hand. It feels soft and warm, too. I wave good-bye to my friends.

At home, I serve us each a bowl of lime sherbet. My mother and I sit on the porch.

"I like your costume, Estelita," says my mother.

"I liked being the only rainbow tulip, *Mamá*," I say, "but it was hard, too."

"It is hard to be different," says my mother. "It's sweet and sour, like your sherbet."

I say, "*Mamá*, tell me again about our family." She tells me about her father, who was a Spanish sea captain, and about her mother, who grew up in Mexico.

"One day I will go," I say. "I will go to Mexico and Spain."

"*Ay, que muchacha*," chuckles my mother, as she pats my hand.

"I will," I say, leaning on my mother, my quiet mother.

We eat our lime sherbet slowly, very slowly.

ABOUT THIS BOOK

"Tell me again about the May parade," I say to my mother when she's in her seventies. She laughs and says, "Oh, about being the rainbow tulip." I turn on the tape recorder and sit back to enjoy Mother's animated face and voice that transport me to the border city of El Paso, Texas, where she, her children, and my children were born.

Mother grew up in the 1920s. Her parents, Sotero Amelia Landavazo and the Mexican circuit judge Eduardo Luis Delgado, had come to El Paso during the Mexican Revolution of 1910.

Between 1880 and the Great Depression, almost one million Mexicans entered the United States. Many arrived first in El Paso, "foreigners in their native land," in the words of historian Ronald Takaki, since until 1848 the land had been Mexican territory. They crossed the desert instead of an ocean. Like my grandparents, many Mexicans remained in this country to become productive citizens, proud of their dual heritage.

I love this photo of my mother as a little girl with her mother, Amelia Delgado, a quiet woman, one of the gentlest women I've ever known.

What pleasure I've had writing a family memoir, listening to the lives of my relatives, to their bilingual voices, their lessons, their songs, their humor. What about you? Have you made a family tree, discovered the treasure of stories that is your family?

— P. M.